MARY POPE OSBORNE'S

TALES FROM THE

ODYSSEY

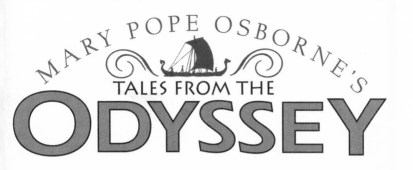

MARY POPE OSBORNE'S
TALES FROM THE
ODYSSEY

Book Three

SIRENS AND
SEA MONSTERS

By **MARY POPE OSBORNE**
With artwork by **TROY HOWELL**

Hyperion Books for Children   New York

Special thanks to Frederick J. Booth, Ph.D.,
Professor of Classical Studies, Seton Hall University,
for his expert advice

First Edition
1 3 5 7 9 10 8 6 4 2
Printed in the United States of America
Library of Congress Cataloging-in-Publication Data on file.
ISBN 0-7868-0772-5
Visit www.hyperionchildrensbooks.com

For Ken Whelan

CONTENTS

PROLOGUE

*I*n the early morning of time, there existed a mysterious world called Mount Olympus. Hidden behind a veil of clouds, this world was never swept by winds, nor washed by rains. Those who lived on Mount Olympus never grew old; they never died. They were not humans. They were the mighty gods and goddesses of ancient Greece.

The Olympian gods and goddesses had great power over the lives of the humans who lived on earth below. Their anger once caused a man named Odysseus to wander the seas for many long years, trying to find his way home.

Almost three thousand years ago, a Greek poet named Homer first told the story of Odysseus' journey. Since that time, storytellers have told the strange and wondrous tale again and again. We call that story the Odyssey.

THE LAND OF THE LIVING

Thousands of wailing ghosts moved toward Odysseus. Their anguished cries echoed through the fog. Odysseus and his men began to run. They ran for their lives, fleeing from the dead. . . .

"Land ahead!" one of Odysseus' men called.

Odysseus woke from his nightmare. He had fallen asleep on the deck of his ship. He had been dreaming of his visit to the spirit world ruled by Hades and Persephone. Now in the distance he could see the island of Circe, the enchantress.

I will tell Circe all that I saw and heard in the Land of the Dead, he thought. *Then surely she will help us find our way home to Ithaca.*

For twelve long years, Odysseus had yearned to return to the Greek island of Ithaca and be reunited with his beloved wife and son. During that time, he and his men had fought in the Trojan War. They had battled the Cyclops, a one-eyed monster. They had escaped cannibal giants, losing all but one of their ships. Odysseus had charmed the wily enchantress Circe, and he and his men had now survived a journey to the Land of the Dead—a journey from which no mortal had ever before returned alive.

As they sailed now toward Circe's sunlit island, the Greeks cheered. The island was covered with beautiful green forests and ringed by rocky shores.

Birds sang in the trees as the Greeks anchored their ship. But as the sun went down and they dragged themselves ashore, a great weariness overtook them. Each man collapsed to the sand, too exhausted to speak.

Lying on the cool beach, Odysseus stared up at the moon and stars. He pushed away all his memories of the Land of the Dead. He felt the soft breezes and listened to the waves lap the shore. The world of the living seemed an extraordinary place indeed.

As rosy-fingered dawn spread over the island, Odysseus opened his eyes.

He saw Circe emerge from her palace. She was dressed in a beautiful gown of rainbow colors. Her handmaidens trailed behind her in the fresh morning air, carrying trays of meat, bread, and wine.

Odysseus jumped to his feet and awakened his men. Then he hurried to greet the goddess. Though the enchantress had once tried to harm him and his men, she was now their friend and protector.

"Greetings!" Odysseus called.

"Welcome, my brave friends!" said

Circe, smiling. "You have done what no other mortals have ever done. You have traveled to the Land of the Dead and returned. When you die, others will say that you have died twice."

"Yes, we are grateful to the gods for our safe journey back to your island," Odysseus said. "We pray that you will now help us find our way home to Ithaca."

"Indeed I will," said Circe. "But today you must rest, for you have a long, hard voyage ahead of you. Feast and drink and celebrate your return. Then tomorrow, when the dawn breaks, you shall set sail for Ithaca."

The men cheered. They were famished and thirsty and delighted to spend the day in the company of Circe and her lovely handmaidens.

All morning and all afternoon, Odysseus and his men feasted and drank wine. When the sun finally set and darkness covered the island, the men lay down in the hollow of their ship and fell fast sleep.

Odysseus himself did not rest. Circe took him by the hand and led him into the moonlit forest. Together they sat in the shadows beneath a towering oak.

"Tell me of your journey, Odysseus," Circe said. "What did you see in the Land of the Dead? What did you learn there?"

Odysseus told Circe about his journey to the gray kingdom of Hades and Persephone, rulers of the dead. He told her about the spirits who had come forth, begging for blood so they might be restored to life.

"Among them was my mother," he said sorrowfully. "She died of grief waiting for me to come home to Ithaca. She told me that my father and my wife and son still ache for my return.

"I spoke also with my friend Achilles, who was slain in the Trojan War. I spoke with the High King, Agamemnon. I saw Heracles, Sisyphus, and Tantalus. Finally I spoke with the blind prophet, Tiresias."

"And what did the prophet tell you?" asked Circe.

"He gave me wise counsel and warnings," said Odysseus. "This is what he said: 'On your way home, you will pass the island of the sun god. On this island there are many beautiful sheep and cattle.

Do not let your men touch even one of these creatures. They are much adored by the sun. Anyone who tries to slay them will meet his doom. You alone might escape. But if you do, you will be a broken man. You will find great trouble in your house.'"

Circe sighed. "Yes, those are wise words," she said. "But before you reach the island of the sun god, you must brave other dangers. Listen to me carefully, Odysseus, for I am about to speak of terrible things. But do exactly as I say, and you and your men will find your way home."

CIRCE'S WARNINGS

"*O*dysseus, can you bear to hear what I have to say?" Circe asked him. "Are you prepared to know of the horrors that await you on your journey?"

Odysseus nodded. What could be more

horrible than the Cyclops, or the cannibal giants—or even the spell Circe herself had once cast on his men, turning them into swine?

Circe began: "Soon after you leave my island, you will come upon the island of the Sirens. The Sirens are beautiful women. From a field of flowers, they sing to all sailors who pass their shores."

Odysseus almost laughed. "What threat could these women possibly be to me and my men?" he asked.

"Any sailor who hears the song of the Sirens will forget his homeland, his wife,

and his children," said Circe. "The Sirens'
lovely singing will lure him to a watery
death."

Odysseus smiled and shook his head.
He could not believe a simple song could
have such power.

"Heed my warning, Odysseus!" said
Circe. "The Sirens' shores are littered with
the bones of sailors driven mad by their
song. You must make your crew plug their
ears with beeswax, so none will be able to
hear. Else you will all perish!"

"I will order them to do so," Odysseus
agreed. "But I myself will listen. I do not

believe my will to return home can be broken by a song."

"Then you alone may hear the Sirens," said Circe. "But first your men must tie your hands and your feet to the mast of the ship, or you will surely hurl yourself into the sea. Tell your men that even if you plead with them to loosen your bonds, they must not. Will you swear to do that?"

Odysseus nodded.

"Once you have sailed past the Sirens, you will see two sea paths," said Circe. "One path will lead you between the Wandering Rocks. The Wandering

Rocks are gigantic boulders that pound against one another with terrific fury. No living thing—not even a dove on her way to Zeus—can pass between them without being crushed.

"The waves that foam about the Wandering Rocks are filled with the wreckage of ships and the bodies of sailors. Only Jason and his Argonauts have survived them, but that was because the goddess Hera loved Jason and protected him."

"I fear we cannot depend upon protection from the gods," said Odysseus.

"Tell me, Circe, what is the other path?"

"The other path leads between two sea cliffs," said Circe. "One cliff is quite low. There, under a great fig tree, dwells the deadly whirlpool monster, Charybdis. Any ship that sails near Charybdis is sucked to the black bottom of the sea. Even Poseidon himself cannot save mortal sailors from the monster whirlpool."

"And what of the other cliff?" asked Odysseus. "What danger lies on its shore?"

"High on the side of the second cliff is a dark cave," said Circe. "In the cave dwells the monster Scylla. She yelps like a small hound. But in truth she is a terrible beast. Even the gods and goddesses cannot look upon her without being sickened."

"Why is she so terrible?" asked Odysseus.

"Scylla is a monster with six huge, hideous heads," said Circe. "Her six mouths are filled with razor-sharp teeth. In an instant, the monster can devour six men. All day, Scylla sits inside her cave, gazing greedily over the sea with her twelve eyes. Whenever a ship sails by, she strikes with all her heads and snatches six sailors from the deck. In no time, she rips her poor victims to pieces."

Odysseus stared at the enchantress. "Then the choice you give me is impossible," he said. "Either we are drowned by the whirlpool monster or we die in the jaws of the six-headed beast."

"The choice is this," Circe said. "If you sail close to the monster whirlpool, you will all die. But if you sail close to Scylla, only six will be lost."

Odysseus closed his eyes. He had already seen dozens of his men die hideous deaths. Some had been eaten by the monstrous Cyclops. Others had been speared alive by cannibal giants. How could he bear to see more slaughtered?

"I counsel you to take the course that leads past the monster Scylla," said Circe. "Do not try to fight her. You will lose six men. But if you sail swiftly enough past the monster, you will lose *only* six. The rest will have a chance to escape."

Odysseus was silent for a moment. He could hardly bear to follow Circe's counsel. "How can I knowingly sacrifice my men to such a hideous death?" he asked. "How can I choose which six will die?"

"It is not in your power to choose who shall die," said Circe. "The monster will make the choice for you. Perhaps she will even choose *you*."

Odysseus shook his head. "No. I will kill her before she touches *any* of us," he said.

"Do not be so proud, Odysseus!" Circe said. "You are only a mortal. No mortal— not even you—can defeat Scylla. While you waste time attacking her with your sword, she will devour another six men.

"You must row your ship at full speed! And shout a prayer to Scylla's mother, asking for help. Only she can stop her savage daughter from devouring more men."

Before Odysseus could protest further, Circe went on.

"If you escape from the monster, it will be time to heed the warnings of Tiresias," Circe said. "For soon you will come to the island of Helios, the sun god. There you will see seven herds of cattle and seven flocks of sheep.

"There are fifty beasts in each herd. They are tended by two fair nymphs, daughters of Helios. The sheep and cattle never give birth. They never die. But if any of your men so much as touches them, all your crew will perish. You yourself might escape, but you will have a sad and terrible time when you return home to your island. Your wife and son will suffer also."

Odysseus stood up. The thought that his family might be in danger kindled his desire to start for home at once. "Thank you for your help," he said to Circe. "I promise to heed your warnings."

"Good," she said. "I have told you all that you need to know. Your path will be dangerous indeed. But if you do as I say, you will find your way home. Go now, for the dawn is almost upon us."

Odysseus looked around at the forest. A misty golden-pink light filtered through the trees. A breeze made the leaves quiver and dance. Birds began to sing.

When Odysseus turned back to the enchantress, she was gone.

"Circe!" he called.

She did not answer. She had slipped away into the dawn's rosy light.

THREE

SONG OF THE SIRENS

Odysseus was eager to set sail. As he hurried back to the shore, Circe's words echoed in his ears: *Your path will be dangerous indeed. But if you do as I say, you will find your way home.*

Odysseus boarded his ship and commanded his men to cast off at once.

The Greeks stumbled from their sleep and took their places at the oars of the black vessel. As Odysseus was about to raise anchor, Circe's handmaidens appeared on the beach. They carried food and wine for the voyage.

The men happily loaded their gifts onto the ship. Then they bade farewell to the fair maidens and pushed off from the shore.

As the ship sailed away from land, Odysseus stared wistfully at the island of the mysterious enchantress. For the past twelve months, Circe had controlled his fate: she had changed his men into swine and back again. She had sent him on an unfathomable journey into the Land of the Dead. She had armed him with prophecies and warnings for his dangerous voyage home.

Even now he could feel her presence as gentle breezes carried his ship across the waves.

❖   ❖   ❖

As his ship sailed onto the open sea, Odysseus thought of Circe's warnings and the dangers he and his men would soon face.

It is not fair, he thought, *that I should know what horrors await us, while my men know nothing.*

Odysseus stood up and called for his crew to listen.

"Friends!" he said. "Circe has told me much about the journey ahead. Now you shall hear her warnings as well. We will soon approach the island of the Sirens. The Sirens are beautiful women who sing from a field of flowers near the sea."

The men laughed, certain they had nothing to fear from lovely singers.

"Take heed," said Odysseus. "Circe has

warned me that any man who hears the song of the Sirens will drown himself trying to get to them. You must plug your ears so that you cannot hear the enchanting song. I alone may listen, but only if you bind my hands and feet so tightly to the mast of the ship that I cannot break loose. If I beg you to set me free, you must bind me tighter still."

As Odysseus spoke, the wind picked up, filling the sail and carrying the black ship faster and faster across the waves. Then, just as suddenly, the wind ceased. The water grew ominously still.

The men looked about with fear.

"Where is the breeze?" one whispered.

"There is not a ripple on the waves," said another. "What has become of the wind?"

"We must be nearing the island of the Sirens," Odysseus said. "Quick! Let down the sail and stow it away! Be silent. Be swift."

The men did as Odysseus commanded. They lowered the sail and stowed it in the hold. Then they picked up their oars and rowed silently through the eerie, still waters.

While the men rowed, Odysseus grabbed a wheel of beeswax. He held the wax in the sun until it was soft, then cut it into many small pieces. He molded the pieces with his fingers, then handed two to each man.

"Use these to keep the song of the Sirens from reaching your ears," he said. "And then you must bind me to the mast."

The men sealed their ears with the wax. Then they took long cords of rope and tied Odysseus to the mast of the ship. They tied the knots so tightly that no man could loosen them.

The Greeks then picked up their oars again and began to row.

As the black ship moved closer to the island, Odysseus began to hear singing waft through the mist. The sound was more beautiful than he had even imagined—high, sweet, and lilting. The words of the Sirens floated on the soft wind:

> *Harken, brave Odysseus,*
> *Listen to us now!*
> *No one can pass our island without staying*
> *To hear our song.*
> *He who listens will be all the wiser,*
> *He who listens*
> *Will discover the secrets of the gods.*

The ship sailed closer and closer to the

shore. Through the mist beyond the still waters, Odysseus saw two lovely women in a flowery meadow.

To his amazement, he saw that the women had wings like birds. Their feathers were translucent in the early morning light.

Odysseus felt an unbearable longing to be with the beautiful creatures. He yearned to spend the rest of his life with them.

As his ship drew closer, Odysseus saw heaps of bleached bones around the bird women. He saw the rotten skin of decaying bodies. He knew he was looking at the remains of sailors who had been enchanted by the Sirens.

But even such a ghastly sight did not keep Odysseus from yearning to throw himself into the sea and swim to the island.

As the Sirens sang their sweet song over and over, Odysseus nearly went mad. He twisted and turned, trying to break free from his bonds.

His men quickened their rowing. Two of them bound Odysseus with more ropes. They rowed faster and faster over the still waters. As they rowed, the song of the Sirens grew fainter.

Odysseus strained to hear the lovely singing as it faded away in the distance. His heart was filled with grief as it grew softer and softer . . . until finally it was gone and all was silent again.

Suddenly the wind picked up. Waves rippled and rolled. Seagulls swooped and cawed.

Odysseus' grief turned to joy. He began to laugh. He was safe! His men were safe! The song of the Sirens was behind them, and they were all safe and well.

THE WHIRLPOOL MONSTER

*W*hen Odysseus' men saw him laughing, they pulled the wax from their ears.

"Untie the ropes!" Odysseus ordered them. "Set me free!"

As his men untied Odysseus, he thanked them.

"I am grateful to you all," he said. "I have heard the song of the Sirens, and I have survived."

The men asked him to describe the beautiful singing. But before Odysseus could speak, he heard a deep rumbling in the distance.

Everyone looked toward the sound. The sea had grown eerily dark. Huge ripples began to rock the ship from side to side.

The rumbling grew louder and louder

until it was a deafening roar. Waves billowed and broke with great force against the ship's hull.

Only Odysseus understood what was happening. His ship and all aboard it were being pulled into the whirlpool of Charybdis.

"Row! Row for your lives!" Odysseus said.

But Odysseus' men shouted in fear and threw down their oars. The ship began to spin in the sea.

Odysseus knew that to escape the whirlpool, he must steer the ship swiftly and steadily toward the cave of the monstrous Scylla. But he could not bear to tell his men the horror that awaited them there.

Instead, Odysseus went around the deck, urging each man not to surrender to fear.

"We have had great trials," he told them, "but we escaped the monstrous Cyclops. We survived the enchantment of Circe. We journeyed to the Land of the Dead and returned unharmed. Pick up your oars now! Row swiftly! Whatever is to come, we must face it with courage!"

Odysseus' heart was heavy as he spoke to his men. He alone knew that at least six of them would soon die hideously in the jaws of the monster Scylla.

Ignorant of their fate and heartened by their leader's words, the Greeks picked up their oars again and began rowing through the wildly rushing waters.

As the helmsman struggled to hold the ship steady, the whirlpool's roar grew unbearably loud. Ferocious waves crashed over the ship.

Soon Odysseus saw a towering cliff looming ahead. The cliff seemed to reach to heaven itself—its peak lost in a cloud. No man could climb to its top, for the cliff's steep sides were as smooth as marble.

Near the cliff's summit was a dark cave. *The home of Scylla, the six-headed monster,* Odysseus thought with dread.

Again Odysseus chose not to tell his men about the monster waiting in her lair. If they knew, their courage would leave them and they would cease to row—and all would be lost in the whirlpool of Charybdis.

Better six shall die than all, Odysseus thought bitterly.

So again, he urged his men to summon their courage:

"Do as I say—trust in Zeus—row with all your might! Steer close to the tall cliff that disappears into the clouds."

Odysseus tried to speak calmly. But he was enraged that six of his comrades were about to die. His fury grew until it led him to make a rash decision: he would defy the counsel of Circe. He would slay the monster before she devoured even one of his men.

Odysseus strapped on his armor. He seized two long spears. Gripping a spear in each hand, he stared up at the looming gray cliff.

Mist partially covered the mouth of Scylla's cave. The cave was so high that even the best warrior could not send an arrow or spear inside it. Odysseus would have to wait for the monster to emerge.

As his men rowed furiously through the dark sea, Odysseus listened for the puppylike yelps of the monster. He waited to see her six long necks and her hideous heads with their rows of gleaming teeth.

He stood on the foredeck of the black ship, ready to slay her.

SCYLLA

s the Greeks drew closer and closer
to Scylla's lair, Odysseus glared fiercely
at her mist-shrouded cave.

But suddenly Odysseus forgot all about
Scylla, for his attention was seized by the

roaring sea. Just off the bow of the ship, the whirlpool monster, Charybdis, was sucking up tons of black water and vomiting it out.

Spray from the monster's mouth rained down on the deck. The sea around the ship bubbled and churned like water roiling in a giant cauldron.

Odysseus could see into the center of the whirlpool—a deep cavity filled with black ooze and mud. If his ship veered even slightly toward the swirling water, it would surely be sucked down into the darkness.

Odysseus dropped his spears. "Hold our course!" he shouted to his men. "Row with all your might toward the towering cliff!"

Odysseus' men cried out in fear. At that moment, Scylla stuck her hideous heads out of her cave.

In an instant, the monster's six long necks swooped down toward the sea. She grabbed Odysseus' best warriors in her six mouths. As she lifted the helpless Greeks high into the air, the men writhed like fish caught by a giant fisherman.

Odysseus saw bloody hands and feet

dangling from Scylla's mouths. He heard the men scream his name, begging for help.

The hideous monster devoured her victims before Odysseus' eyes. It was the most terrible sight of his life.

Odysseus knew now that Circe had been right. He had been foolish to think he could slay the monster. The only way to save the rest of his men was to speed away from her as swiftly as possible.

"Row! Row!" he shouted. "If you value your lives, row with all your strength!"

The men rowed frantically past the tall cliff. With Odysseus urging them on, they sped through the channel, until they were finally safe from both sea monsters, Scylla and Charybdis.

SIX

ISLAND OF THE SUN GOD

*O*dysseus stood at the helm of his ship. He stared into the churning sea behind him, horrified by the cruel slaughter of his men. Their screams still rang in his ears. The sight of their bloody, struggling limbs was imprinted on his memory forever.

But Odysseus knew that the rest of his men needed him now—their fear and trembling forced him to rally himself and take command.

"Row on!" he said, lifting his head in the wind. "Do not look back! Do not think about what you have seen, or we will never find our way home!"

Too stunned even to speak, the Greeks picked up their oars. Like obedient children, they rowed on.

The black ship sped across the wine-dark

sea. Soon the Greeks saw a sun-drenched island in the distance. They heard the lowing of cattle and bleating of sheep.

Odysseus' men rejoiced at the sounds. After their terrible ordeal, they yearned for rest and shelter and food.

"Soon we will feast on beef and mutton!" they exclaimed.

Odysseus did not rejoice. He knew that he and his men were approaching the island of the sun god. He remembered the stern warnings of the prophet Tiresias and the counsel of Circe.

"Heed what I tell you," he said to his

crew. "I know you crave food and rest. But the island ahead belongs to Helios, the sun god. We cannot seek provisions there. I have been warned by the prophet Tiresias and by Circe. They told me that the sun god adores his cattle and sheep, and that if one of you even dares touch them, you all will die."

Upon hearing these words, the men nearly collapsed with weariness and anguish.

"Then let us die there," said one, "for we will surely die at sea if we do not eat and rest soon."

"Listen to me," Odysseus said. "If we stop now, all our trials—all our triumphs and all our losses—will have been for naught. We must move past this island. We must keep rowing."

The men protested again. When Odysseus would not hear their pleas, Eurylochus, the second in command on the ship, shouted at him in anger.

"Odysseus, you are too strong!" he said. "You are made of iron; the rest of us are not! We are only human. These men need rest from their labor and time to mourn their losses. They cannot row through the night. Let us heed the darkness. Let us stop on the island to rest. We will cook our own food and sleep on the sand. We will set sail again at dawn without even laying eyes upon the precious cattle and sheep of the sun god."

The men cheered the plan put forth by Eurylochus, but Odysseus' heart was filled with dread. Even though the plan seemed sound, Odysseus felt as if some angry god were plotting against him. Still, he knew there was no way now he could convince his men to row on.

"You force me to surrender to your

will," he said. "I cannot fight you all. But if we do as Eurylochus asks, you must swear an oath—you must promise not to touch a single head of the sun god's cattle or sheep. You must be satisfied only with the food that Circe has given us."

The men swore to do as Odysseus commanded. Soon they dropped anchor in a sheltered bay of Helios' island.

Near the shore, the Greeks found a spring of fresh water. They set up camp and made a meal from Circe's gifts of meat and bread and wine.

Once the men had satisfied their hunger and thirst, painful memories swept over them. They wept for their six comrades eaten alive by the monster Scylla. Her victims had been the strongest and best of Odysseus' warriors.

The Greeks wept also for the others on their voyage who had been slain by monsters and giants. They mourned their losses deep into the night, until sleep mercifully overcame them.

SEVEN

THE TEMPEST

*I*n the darkest period of the night, just before the dawn, Zeus sent a terrible storm to the island of the sun god. Fierce winds shook the trees. Cold rain poured down from the heavens.

The Greeks scrambled into a huge cave near the shore. They huddled together, listening to the roar of the storm. At the first light of dawn, as the wind and rain raged on, Odysseus ordered his men to drag their ship ashore and pull it into the cave with them.

Once the ship was safely in the cave, Odysseus gathered his crew around him.

"Friends, we cannot leave the island this morning," he told them. "So I command you again: do not touch the sheep or cows that belong to Helios, the sun god. He sees all and he hears all. He will know at once if you try to feast upon his treasures. We have all the food we need now in our ship. As soon as this tempest ends, we will sail on."

The Greek warriors promised to do as Odysseus commanded. But day after day, fierce storm winds from the south and east pummeled the sun god's island. The days grew into weeks, and still the tempest did not end. Never did the storm cease long enough for the Greeks to set sail.

For over a month, Odysseus and his men remained stranded on the island. At first, they ate only the food given them by

Circe. But when those provisions were gone, the men were forced to roam the stormy coast, spearing fish and birds and anything else they might eat.

As the tempest raged on and on, Odysseus and his men could not find enough food. Each day, they ate less. Each day, they grew weaker. Hunger gnawed at their bellies and despair seized their souls.

Odysseus grew more and more frightened that the men would lose control of themselves. He feared their hunger would eventually drive them to slay the cattle and sheep of the sun god. And he knew that the sun god's anger would bring death upon them all.

Early one morning while the others were still sleeping, Odysseus slipped from the cave. He ran through the storm and took shelter in a solitary outcropping of rock near the shore.

Odysseus knelt on the ground. He raised his arms and called out to the gods and goddesses of Mount Olympus. He begged them to show pity: "Give us courage to withstand our hunger and despair," he prayed. "Send us fair weather so we might sail away soon. Help us

follow the counsel of Tiresias and over-
come temptation. . . ."

As Odysseus prayed, a great drowsi-
ness overtook him. He closed his eyes. His
head fell forward and he sank into a deep,
dreamless sleep.

PUNISHMENT OF THE GODS

*O*dysseus woke with a start. He could tell from the morning light that several hours had passed since he had fallen asleep. With a feeling of dread, he leapt from the ground and started running back to his men.

As Odysseus neared the cave, his heart sank. The smell of burning meat filled the air.

Odysseus was seized with rage and horror. Rushing into the cave, he grabbed the first man he came upon. "What have you done?" he demanded. "Have you disobeyed my orders and defied the gods?"

"We were following Eurylochus!" the man said. "He told us that starvation was the most terrible of all deaths! He urged us to slay the cattle of the sun god! He said we could appease Helios by building a great temple in his honor when we return to Ithaca."

Odysseus nearly wept with despair.

"We were so hungry, we could not stop ourselves," the man said. "We killed the best of the cattle and roasted them over the fire."

Odysseus cried out in agony. He fell to his knees and called to the gods: "Zeus and all immortal gods, why did you allow me to fall asleep? I begged you to give my men strength and courage! Now they have defied my command and slain the cattle of Helios! Have mercy on us! Have mercy on us all!"

But Odysseus knew his prayers were in vain. The rage of Helios was surely more powerful than the anguished pleas of a mere mortal. Odysseus imagined that the sun god might threaten never to shine upon the earth again unless the gods helped him take his revenge.

Odysseus rose to his feet and looked about the cave. The scene was horrible and unnatural. The hides of the slain cattle crawled across the ground. On the spits, the roasting meat bellowed like living beasts.

Odysseus' men cowered before him. As he glared at their terrified faces, the rage drained from his heart. It was too late for rage now. The cattle of Helios were dead, and the men who had slain them would soon die also. Nothing less, Odysseus knew, would appease the sun god's anger.

❖　❖　❖

For the next six days, as the winds blew harshly outside the cave, Odysseus' men feasted on the sun god's cattle.

Finally, on the seventh day, the storm abruptly ceased.

At Odysseus' command, the Greeks pulled their ship from its shelter and pushed off into the water. A gentle west wind caught their sail, and they headed once again for the distant shores of Ithaca.

For a time, it seemed possible that the sun god's rage had been forgotten. But once the black ship had sailed onto the open sea, Odysseus' worst fears were realized. Helios had indeed turned all the other gods against the Greeks. And together, the gods took their revenge.

First, mighty Zeus sent a black storm cloud across the sky, darkening the waters and turning the day into night.

Then Poseidon, god of the seas, sent tumultuous waves crashing over the sides of the ship.

Then Aeolus, the wind god, sent a howling wind that blew with such fury that it cracked the ship's mast. The mast and rigging fell on top of the helmsman, crushing his skull.

Zeus shook the sky with thunder and hurled down a blazing bolt of lightning. The lightning struck the ship's hull, spinning it around and around on the water. All of Odysseus' men were thrown from the deck into the dark, angry sea.

Watching helplessly from the ship, Odysseus saw his men tossed on the waves like sea birds. He watched as, one by one, they sank beneath the water and drowned.

Finally all of Odysseus' men had disappeared under the waves. And Odysseus was completely and terribly alone.

ONLY ODYSSEUS

*O*dysseus clung to the lurching ship until the storm began to rip it apart. Then, as the rest of the ship was torn to splinters, he lashed the mast and keel together, making a raft.

For hours, Odysseus clung to the raft for dear life as wild winds tossed him over the waves.

Darkness soon covered the ocean. As the sea grew calmer, Odysseus feared his raft might be drifting back toward the cave of Scylla and the whirlpool of Charybdis. All through the night he prayed to the gods to spare him from the monsters.

But as dawn broke, Odysseus saw Scylla's cliff rising from the sea—and he heard the awful roar of Charybdis. He could feel the black waters of Charybdis' whirlpool begin to pull at his raft.

Odysseus' prayers had been in vain. His raft was being sucked into the black, swirling mouth of Charybdis. His body would soon join those of all the other sailors who had drowned in the terrible whirlpool.

But just as he was about to be sucked into the monster's mouth, a mighty wave swept Odysseus from his raft. The wave carried him away from the whirlpool— over the sea—onto the shores of Scylla's cliff.

Odysseus flung himself from the water and grabbed the trunk of a huge fig tree. He clung to the tree like a bat. Holding on with all his strength, he waited for the whirlpool monster to vomit up his raft.

Finally the raft was hurled from the black abyss and sent swirling over the waves. When it was within reach, Odysseus let go of the tree and plunged into the sea.

He grabbed the edge of the raft and heaved himself aboard. Then he began rowing madly with his hands. He rowed and rowed. He rowed away from Charybdis. He rowed past the cliff of

Scylla. He rowed until he was safe from both dreaded sea monsters.

※　　※　　※

For nine days and nine nights, Odysseus drifted on his raft. He had no food and no water. He had no idea where he was going—or how he would ever get home.

As he drifted over the open sea, he mourned the loss of all his comrades. He grieved for the family he feared he would never see again.

Finally, on the tenth day, the waves tossed Odysseus and his raft onto the shore of a mysterious island.

CALYPSO

*O*dysseus lay on the sandy beach, tired to the bone and filled with despair. He had not slept in ten days. Now that he was safe on shore, he was tortured by visions of his men dangling from the mouths of the monstrous Scylla. Over and over he saw his comrades devoured by monsters or drowned in the waves, bobbing like sea birds, then vanishing, one by one. Friends and warriors, men he had journeyed with for twelve long years—they were now gone. He had lost them all.

Only the last words of Tiresias, the blind prophet, were yet to come to pass: *"You alone might escape. But if you do, you will be a broken man. You will find great trouble in your house."*

Odysseus could not bear the thought that Penelope, his wife, and Telemachus, his son, might be suffering in Ithaca. He desperately wanted to protect them. In spite of his despair, he still felt a fierce determination to return home.

Nearly blind with exhaustion and grief, Odysseus pulled himself up from the sand and began walking in search of help.

He had not gone far before he came upon four streams. The bubbling waters wound through lush green meadows filled with violets, parsley, and wild celery.

Just beyond the streams was a rocky hillside. Set deep in the rocks was a huge cave. Long vines trailed around the mouth of the cave. Clusters of ripe grapes hung from the vines.

Beautiful trees grew along the path that led to the cave—alder, aspen, and sweet-smelling cypress. Owls, falcons, and sea ravens had built their nests in the boughs of the trees.

Odysseus smelled the sweet scent of burning cedar and sandalwood.

Like someone lost in a dream, Odysseus stumbled slowly toward the cave's entrance. When he peered inside, he saw a great fire blazing in the hearth.

Beside the hearth sat a beautiful woman

at a loom. She shone with the light of a goddess. She was weaving and singing in a lovely voice.

As her song ended, the goddess turned and smiled at Odysseus.

"Hello, Odysseus," she said. "I am Calypso, daughter of Atlas. Hermes told me that you might come."

Odysseus was surprised that the goddess knew his name. But he was too weary even to speak.

Calypso looked at Odysseus for a long time. Then she continued in her calm, lovely voice: "I know what has happened to you," she said. "Your men killed the cattle of the sun god. In a rage, Helios threatened to take away his light forever, from men and from the gods. Zeus and the other gods of Mount Olympus were forced to take revenge against you. Zeus smashed your ship with a thunderbolt and hurled your warriors into the sea. They drowned before your eyes."

Odysseus nodded.

"You must be very tired, Odysseus," Calypso said kindly. "Come inside. Rest here in my home."

Without a word, Odysseus stepped

into the cave of the beautiful goddess.

He stumbled to the hearth and lay down close to the fire. After his terrible journey, he was indeed a broken man. His heart and body ached almost more than he could bear.

As Odysseus stared at the fire in the hearth, the goddess began to sing her song again. Odysseus was reminded of the singing of the Sirens. But Calypso's song did not make him go mad or lure him to a watery death.

Instead, as Odysseus listened, all the pain and horror of his journey slowly dissolved around him. He felt peaceful and calm for the first time in many weeks.

Odysseus closed his eyes. And in the peaceful warmth of Calypso's cave, he finally fell asleep.

ABOUT HOMER AND THE ODYSSEY

Long ago, the ancient Greeks believed that the world was ruled by a number of powerful gods and goddesses. Stories about the gods and goddesses are called the Greek myths. The myths were probably first told as a way to explain things in nature—such as weather, volcanoes, and constellations. They were also recited as entertainment.

The first written record of the Greek

myths comes from a blind poet named Homer. Homer lived almost three thousand years ago. Many believe that Homer was the author of the world's two most famous epic poems: the *Iliad* and the *Odyssey*. The *Iliad* is the story of the Trojan War. The *Odyssey* tells about the long journey of Odysseus, king of an island called Ithaca. The tale concerns Odysseus' adventures on his way home from the Trojan War.

To tell his tales, Homer seems to have drawn upon a combination of his own imagination and Greek myths that had been passed down by word of mouth. A bit of actual history may have also gone into Homer's stories; there is archaeological evidence to suggest that the story of the Trojan War was based on a war fought about five hundred years before Homer's time.

Over the centuries, Homer's *Odyssey* has greatly influenced the literature of the Western world.

GODS AND GODDESSES OF ANCIENT GREECE

The most powerful of all the Greek gods and goddesses was Zeus, the thunder god. Zeus ruled the heavens and the mortal world from a misty mountaintop known as Mount Olympus. The main Greek gods and goddesses were all relatives of Zeus. His brother Poseidon was ruler of the seas, and his brother Hades was ruler of the underworld. His wife Hera was queen of the gods and goddesses. Among his many children were the gods Apollo, Mars, and Hermes, and the goddesses Aphrodite, Athena, and Artemis.

The gods and goddesses of Mount Olympus not only inhabited their mountaintop but also visited the earth, involving themselves in the daily activities of mortals such as Odysseus.

THE MAIN GODS
AND GODDESSES
AND PRONUNCIATION
OF THEIR NAMES

Zeus (zyoos), king of the gods, god of thunder

Poseidon (poh-SY-don), brother of Zeus, god of seas and rivers

Hades (HAY-deez), brother of Zeus, king of the Land of the Dead

Hera (HEE-ra), wife of Zeus, queen of the gods and goddesses

Hestia (HES-tee-ah), sister of Zeus, goddess of the hearth

Athena (ah-THEE-nah), daughter of Zeus, goddess of wisdom and war, arts and crafts

Demeter (dee-MEE-tur), goddess of crops and the harvest, mother of Persephone

Aphrodite (ah-froh-DY-tee), daughter of Zeus, goddess of love and beauty

Artemis (AR-tem-is), daughter of Zeus, goddess of the hunt

Ares (AIR-eez), son of Zeus, god of war

Apollo (ah-POL-oh), god of the sun, music, and poetry

Hermes (HUR-meez), son of Zeus, messenger god, a trickster

Hephaestus (heh-FEES-tus), son of Hera, god of the forge

Persephone (pur-SEF-oh-nee), daughter of Zeus, wife of Hades and queen of the Land of the Dead

Dionysus (dy-oh-NY-sus), god of wine and madness

PRONUNCIATION GUIDE TO
OTHER PROPER NAMES

Achilles (ah-KIL-eez)

Aeolus (EE-oh-lus)

Agamemnon (ag-ah-MEM-non)

Calypso (Kah-LIP-soh)

Charybdis (Kah-RIB-dis)

Circe (SIR-see)

Cyclops (SY-klops)

Eurylochus (yoo-RIH-loh-kus)

Helios (HE-lee-ohs)

Heracles (HER-ah-Kleez)

Ithaca (ITH-ah-kah)

Odysseus (oh-DIS-yoos)

Penelope (pen-EL-oh-pee)

Polyphemus (pah-lih-FEE-mus)

Scylla (SIL-ah)

Sisyphus (SIS-ih-fus)

Tantalus (TAN-tah-lus)

Telemachus (tel-EM-ah-kus)

Tiresias (ty-REE-sih-us)

Trojans (TROH-junz)

A NOTE ON THE SOURCES

$\mathcal{T}$he story of the *Odyssey* was originally written down in the ancient Greek language. Since that time there have been countless translations of Homer's story into other languages. I consulted a number of English translations, including those written by Alexander Pope, Samuel Butler, Andrew Lang, W.H.D. Rouse, Edith Hamilton, Robert Fitzgerald, Allen Mandelbaum, and Robert Fagles.

Homer's *Odyssey* is divided into twenty-four books. The third volume of *Tales from the Odyssey* was derived from book twelve of Homer's *Odyssey*, with details concerning Odysseus' arrival on Calypso's island coming from book five.

ABOUT THE AUTHOR

MARY POPE OSBORNE is the author of the best-selling Magic Tree House series. She has also written many acclaimed historical novels and retellings of myths and folktales, including *Kate and the Beanstalk* and *New York's Bravest*. She lives with her husband in New York City and Connecticut.

Zeus

Hera

Artemis

Hephaestus

Apollo

Athena

Ares